# TOMMY DONBAVAND'S FUNNY SHORTS

# THE CURIOUS CASE OF THE PANICKY PARROT

WRITTEN BY TOMMY DONBAVAND
ILLUSTRATED BY KEN McFARLANE

EDGE
FRANKLIN WATTS

LONDON·SYDNEY

Franklin Watts
First published in Great Britain in 2017 by The Watts Publishing Group

Credits
Executive Editor: Adrian Cole
Design Manager: Peter Scoulding
Cover Designer: Cathryn Gilbert
Illustrations: Ken McFarlane

HB ISBN 978 1 4451 5256 1
PB ISBN 978 1 4451 5258 5
Library ebook ISBN 978 1 4451 5257 8

Printed in China.

MIX
Paper from
responsible sources
FSC
www.fsc.org   FSC® C104740

Franklin Watts
An imprint of
Hachette Children's Group
Part of The Watts Publishing Group
Carmelite House
50 Victoria Embankment
London EC4Y 0DZ

An Hachette UK Company
www.hachette.co.uk

www.franklinwatts.co.uk

3 8043 27160297 7

# CONTENTS

# CHAPTER ONE
## CLiENT

The dame entered my office the way a hungry penguin walks into a fishmongers — without knocking. She didn't have an appointment, but gals like her don't need one. I looked her up and down. She frowned, as if she'd lost her sense of humour. I hoped she didn't expect me to find it.

She sat at the other side of my desk, wearing an expression that said she'd won a year's supply of milk, but it had all gone bad the following day. Maybe that's why she was such a sour puss.

Suddenly, the dame pounced — snatching my diary from my paw, and flicking through the pages.

"Hey!" I cried. "I was writing in that!"

"Dame?" exclaimed Tray with a scowl. "You call me a dame in your diary?"

Pouch shrugged. "I'm a private detective. That's how detectives talk."

"In old black-and-white movies, maybe," said Tray. "And may I remind you that this is my office as well as yours? We're partners."

"Yeah," agreed Pouch, "but my name's first on the door ..."

The dog pointed to the lettering on the frosted glass, reversed now the door to the office was closed.

Tray narrowed her feline eyes. "That's because you painted it!"

Pouch shrugged. "I can't help it if 'Tray and Pouch Investigations' doesn't sound right, but 'Pouch and Tray' does."

"Whatever!" sighed Tray, tossing Pouch his diary. "What's on the agenda for today?"

As if in response, a tiny flap near the bottom of the door flipped open and a small mouse in a pink dress scuttled in, clutching some miniature files.

"Your nine o'clock is here," it squeaked.

"Thanks, Doris," said Tray as a long, green, yellow and black snake slithered in through the hatch. The creature stretched its mouth open wide as it made a lunge for the mouse.

With a growl, Pouch leapt across the desk and landed on the end of the snake's tail. It cried out in pain, and pulled away from Doris.

The mouse smiled up at him. "Thanks, boss!" she peeped. "You saved my life."

"Don't mention it," replied Pouch. "Good secretaries are hard to find."

Doris pushed her tiny glasses up her nose, then scampered back through the flap.

Once she was out of harm's reach, Tray stooped to address the newcomer. "My partner will release you now," she snarled. "But if you try anything like that again, we won't be responsible for our actions."

The snake nodded. "I'm sorry," she croaked. "It was instinct. I've come to hire the famed detectives, Pouch and Tray."

"Oops!" said Pouch, releasing the reptile. "If I'd known you were a potential client—"

"—you'd have done exactly the same thing," Tray finished.

"Yeah!" growled Pouch. "Because I'm a terror!"

"No," sighed Tray. "You're a terrier!"

"Oh, yeah," said Pouch, taking his seat and grabbing a pencil. "I must write that down ..."

The cat eased herself back into her own chair. "You've found Tray and Pouch—"

"Pouch and Tray!" her partner muttered under his breath.

"Who are you, and what do you want?" demanded the cat.

"My name's Coral, and I'm here about my husband," the snake sniffed, tears trickling down her scaly skin.

"What about him?" Tray asked, passing the snake a tissue.

"Freddie used to be so chatty," explained Coral, taking the tissue with her tail and dabbing at her eyes. "In fact, it's the thing he's known for."

"Tray says that about me, too!" interrupted Pouch. "There was one time—"

An angry stare quickly had the dog concentrating on his diary again.

Coral wrung out the tissue. "But, then something happened. Something that must have scared him. And now ... now he's ..."

"He's what?" asked Tray.

Coral flicked out her forked tongue to steady her nerves. "He's disappeared!"

# CHAPTER TWO
## CLUE

The detectives climbed the steps to the
door of Coral and Freddie's house.

"Think we'll find any clues?" asked Pouch.

"I hope so," said Tray. "At the moment,
we've got nothing to go on."

Pouch grinned. "Good job I went before
we left the office, then," he said. "And yes,
I flushed and washed my paws."

Tray lifted her own paw to knock on the
door, then realised it was open slightly.

She gave it a push, and it swung inward with an eerie CRRRREEEEAAAAAKK!

"Well, nothing there!" exclaimed Pouch, heading back down the stairs. "Too bad."

Tray grabbed the collar of his raincoat to stop him. "I thought you were a terrier."

"Terrier-fied, more like!" croaked Pouch.

"Follow me ..." said Tray, stepping inside.

"Must I?" whimpered Pouch.

"No," replied Tray. "You can stay here and keep watch, if you like. Just let me know if any murderers turn up."

Pouch was beside her in a flash. "I can't let you go in there alone and without back up," he insisted, grabbing the handle of the first interior door they came to. "We're partners, remember?" He counted quietly to three. Then to six. And then on to twenty-five.

Tray pushed past him and entered the room. Inside was a sofa, an armchair, and a long pole that hung from the ceiling by two lengths of chain.

"Cool!" said Pouch. "They've got a swing in their lounge!"

"That's not a swing," said Tray. "It's a
perch. It must be where Freddie sits."

Pouch frowned. "Why would he sit on
a swing — sorry, perch?"

Tray gestured to a few sheets of newspaper
and a handful of brightly coloured feathers
beneath the perch. "Coral didn't tell us,

"Coral didn't tell us, but I'm guessing Freddie is some kind of bird. Probably a parrot by the look of these feathers."

She picked up one of the colourful feathers and studied it.

"And he's still missing," said Pouch. "So, what now?"

Tray tucked the feather inside her raincoat. "We go to see another bird ..."

They found the pigeon rifling through a bin in an alley. "Hey, Stool," said Tray as she and Pouch approached. "Long time, no see."

"Aw, man!" groaned Stool, abandoning his search of the bin's contents and hopping down to the cracked pavement. "What do youse two want now?"

"The same as always," said the cat. "Information."

"Yeah? Well, I'm fresh out!"

"Is that right?" demanded Pouch. He plunged his fist into his raincoat pocket and produced a pawful of seed, which he scattered on the ground.

Stool tried to control himself, but the hunger was too much and he bent to devour

the food. "Hey, how 'bout that? I just found
a fresh batch of information out back," he
said once he'd finished. "What do youse
wanna know?"

Tray pulled the feather from inside her
coat. "Take a look at this ..."

Stool took the feather and studied it. "A bit flashy for my tastes."

"I'm not interested in what it looks like," said Tray. "It's the smell …"

Stool held the feather up to his nostrils and sniffed. "Wowee!" he cried. "That's some exotic scent!"

Tray nodded. "And it's not the brand of perfume this guy's wife wore to our office," she said. "I want to know who does."

"I'd love to help," said Stool. "I really would, but—"

Pouch scattered more seed on the ground.

"All right," said Stool, lowering his voice and checking up and down the alley to ensure no-one was listening in. "There's this

DJ, works in a nightclub downtown. This is her favourite perfume. She has it imported."

Tray opened her notebook. "You got a name?"

"Of course he does — everyone does!" said Pouch. "Mine's Pouch Goodboy!"

Tray sighed. "The name of the DJ."

"Oh," said Pouch. "Sorry, I've no idea."

Stool lowered his voice even further. "Her name is Arizona. She works at Stingers, but I wouldn't go there if I were youse."

Tray frowned. "Why not?"

A look of fear flashed across Stool's eyes. "Because the place is owned by the most dangerous mob boss this city has ever known ... The Dogfather."

# CHAPTER THREE
## CLUB

As Pouch and Tray pushed open the door to Stingers nightclub, a black-suited goat stepped into their path.

"We ain't open," he bleated.

"You are for us," said Tray, side-stepping the security guard and striding onwards.

Pouch hurried after her, pausing only to wave at the goat. "Hello!"

The club was almost empty, aside from a small group gathered at the bar, and a handful of skunks dancing to loud, pumping punk music.

Tray made straight for a well-dressed Pug, sitting on one of the bar stools. Two chunky bulldogs growled at her.

"You want me to throw these guys out, boss?" asked the goat, hurrying in.

"Nah," said the Pug. "The detectives are welcome here anytime."

Clearly disappointed, the goat turned to make his way back to his post.

"Here's looking at you, kid!" Pouch called after him.

Tray eyed the mob boss suspiciously.

"You know who we are?" she asked.

The pug smiled. "I know who everybody

is, baby." He glanced over at his

bodyguards, both still snorting with fury.

"Miff! Vex! That's enough!"

Reluctantly, the pair of bulldogs stopped

snarling.

"I'm not your baby," said Tray, flatly.

"And I'm not a criminal," said the pug.

"So, to what do I owe the pleasure?"

Tray fixed the dog with a hard stare. "You must be Don Puggini. The Dogfather."

"Are you sure?"

"As sure as I am that these two aren't Batman and Robin," said Tray, gesturing to the two bulldogs. They started to growl again, only quieter this time.

"We're looking for Arizona," said Pouch.

The Dogfather nodded. "Nice holiday spot," he said. "You turn left at Colorado, then go straight on through New Mexico. Send me a postcard when you get there."

"We will," grinned Pouch, pulling out his notebook again. "What's your address? OW!"

He bent to rub at where Tray had kicked his shin.

"You know exactly who we mean," said the cat, pointing towards the dance floor where the skunks were now dancing to some soul funk. "Arizona is the name of a DJ who works here."

"I just own this place," said Don Puggini. "My manager, Sheldon, hires the talent."

"Then we'd like to speak with him," said Pouch.

"I'm afraid that won't be possible," said the pug. "Sheldon is sleeping with the fishes."

Pouch's eyes grew wide. "You mean he's ... dead?"

"What?" exclaimed The Dogfather. "No! He lives in an aquarium across town. He was up all night, so I sent him home to get some rest. Mind you, that's not easy with a horse's head in your bed."

"A horse's head?" Pouch gasped.

"And an entire horse's body."

Tray frowned. "A horse's head and a horse's body in his bed? So ... a horse, then?"

Don Puggini nodded. "His wife, Winnie. She wants a divorce, but Sheldon won't agree to it. So, I guess she's saddled with him."

"Why was he up all night?" asked Tray. "This place closes at 2 a.m."

"We had a break-in around a week ago," The Dogfather explained. "Sheldon has been staying late after work since then to make certain the club is secure."

"Was anything taken?"

"You're not working for the cops?"

Tray shook her head. "We're on a missing person case."

"OK," said the pug. "Our visitor stole a diamond from my safe. The Blue Moo."

Pouch whistled. "That's an extremely

29

rare gem," he said. "Worth around twelve million dollars." He caught Tray's astonished expression. "What? I do know some stuff!"

Tray turned her attention back to The Dogfather. "Twelve million dollars, and you don't want to talk to the police?"

"Let's just say I acquired The Blue Moo in

circumstances they might not appreciate," said Don Puggini, leaping down from his seat. "Now, if there's nothing else ..."

"Actually, there is," said Tray. "We'd like to see your security footage."

"Help yourself," said The Dogfather. Then he made for a windowed office at the back of the club. "Boys!"

Miff and Vex scurried after their boss. Once inside the office with him, one of the two bulldogs lowered the window blinds, obscuring the detectives' view.

"He was nice," Tray commented.

"I didn't think so," said Pouch, missing her sarcastic tone, "and we won't get anything from his footage." He pointed to a shelf high up in the corner of the room, where a goldfish was swimming around in a bowl. "They only have enough memory for about thirty seconds."

"Oi!" gurgled the goldfish. "That's a myth. We goldfish can remember stuff for much longer than thirty seconds!"

"Really?" said Pouch. "How long?"

The goldfish sniffed. "I'm up to almost two minutes now."

Tray sighed. "Still no good. Freddie hasn't been seen for a week."

"Don Puggini has been promising to get the elephant upgrade," said a voice behind them. "But it doesn't cost peanuts."

The pair turned to see a scorpion with a

pierced sting walking towards them.

"Are you here about the break in?"

"We may be," said Tray. "That depends
on who you are."

The scorpion smiled broadly. "My name
is Arizona."

# CHAPTER FOUR
## CLIMB

No-one said a word until they slid into
a booth at a nearby coffee shop. The
hedgehog waitress poured Tray a cup of
steaming, black liquid, while Pouch
pulled out his notebook.

"We're looking for a parrot called
Freddie," said Tray. "He's not been
seen for a while."

"Freddie's missing?" Arizona exclaimed.
"He's a pretty boy. And kind, too.

He wouldn't hurt a fly."

Pouch licked the tip of his pencil.

"Does this fly work at Stingers, too?"

Arizona nodded. "His name's Kevin.
He's the janitor."

"So, you admit to knowing Freddie?"
asked Tray.

"Everyone at Stingers does," said Arizona. "He's a regular, but he hasn't been in lately."

"Since the night of the robbery, possibly?"

Arizona gasped. "How did you know that?"

"Because we think he witnessed the theft," Tray said. "We're hoping he's gone into hiding, and the culprit hasn't found a way to keep him silent."

Pouch glanced up from his notepad. "Or, he could be as dead as some doodoo."

"It's dodo," Tray corrected.

"Dodo doodoo?" said Pouch, screwing up his nose. "Euew!"

"If you all know Freddie, how come he only had your perfume on his feathers?"

Arizona's cheeks flushed. "We ... we sometimes had a dance together," she admitted. "It was nothing serious, I promise."

"What kind of dance?" Pouch asked. "Disco? Ballroom? Gangnam style?"

"Just a normal dance!" Arizona insisted. "That night ... it was almost closing time. I put on a slow song, Freddie wrapped his wings around me, and we ... danced!"

"And that's when the robbery took place?"

"I think so," replied Arizona. "I was facing the opposite direction, but Freddie was looking towards Don Puggini's office, and the blinds were up. Freddie must have seen everything."

"You don't know the identity of the thief?"

"I'm sorry, no," said the scorpion.

"Well, that got us nowhere fast!" moaned Pouch, snapping his notebook shut. He made to slip it back inside his raincoat, but Tray grabbed his wrist. "What's that?" she demanded.

"It's a notebook," said Pouch. "You've got one too, remember?"

"Not that!" said Tray. "The thing you're

using as a bookmark."

   She plucked what appeared to be a
strip of dark plastic from between the
notepad's pages.

"Hey!" cried Pouch. "Now I've lost my place!"

"Where did you get this?" demanded Tray, turning the bookmark over in her hands.

"I found it on our way out of Stingers," said Pouch. "Why?"

"This is a piece of skin," said Tray. She focused her attention back to Arizona. "Scorpions can shed their skin …"

"How dare you?" snapped Arizona. "Stingers is not that kind of club!"

"Then, whose skin is it?" questioned Pouch.

"I don't know," said Tray. "But I know someone who will … Come on, let's go."

Tray dug her claws into the soft bark and began to climb the tree. Pouch hung on to her tail, catching a free ride to wherever his partner was going.

Eventually, they reached a large nest in the uppermost branches, and clambered inside. The interior was packed with all manner of scientific equipment: test tubes, microscopes, sampling machines and more.

Engrossed in a string of numbers crawling across a screen was a big, brown buzzard.

"Excuse me," said Tray. "Are you Stephen Hawk?"

The bird looked up, surprised that he had company. "Do I know you?"

"My name is Tray. I believe you knew my father, Furlock Holmes."

"Oh, yes!" said Stephen, his beak melting into a smile. "I should have known — you have his eyes. How is old Furlock these days?"

"Retired," said Tray. "But he keeps himself busy, chasing red dots, and so on."

"Do give him my best," said the buzzard. "Now, what can I do for you?"

Tray handed over the piece of skin.

"What can you tell me about this?"

Stephen Hawk took the scrap and slid

it under the lens of his microscope. "It's

skin," he said, peering into the eyepiece,

"but I guess you had already deduced that.

Who shed it?"

"I think it might be from a scorpion DJ who works at a nightclub," said Tray.

Stephen Hawk picked up the flap of skin and handed it back. "I'm afraid you're wrong, Miss Holmes," he said. "That is not scorpion skin."

Tray raised her eyebrows. "Are you sure?"

"Absolutely," said the buzzard, firmly. "That piece of skin came from a snake!"

# CHAPTER FIVE
## CLOSED

A female horse slowly opened the door to the aquarium. "Can I help you?" she asked.

Tray handed over her calling card. "We're detectives Tray and Pouch," she said. "Can we come in and ask you some questions?"

"Of course," replied the horse, stepping aside.

Pouch and Tray walked into a room lined from floor to ceiling with water-filled tanks, each containing a number of brightly coloured tropical fish.

"Do you ever get the feeling you're being watched?" he asked his partner.

Tray glanced over at the tanks where every single fish had stopped swimming to peer at them through the glass. Noticing the cat looking, they all turned and swam away quickly, sending streams of bubbles cascading to the surface.

"My name is Winnie," said the horse, shifting from hoof to hoof. "Freddie's not here."

"How do you know we're looking for Freddie McCaw?" said Tray, turning to Winnie.

"Did I say Freddie?" said the horse,

whinnying nervously. "I haven't seen him recently. I was in hospital until yesterday."

Pouch produced his notebook. "Why were you in horse-pital?"

"I fell and hurt my leg, galloping for the bus."

"Was it serious?" asked Tray.

Winnie nodded. "Yes, but I was in a stable condition. Listen, I'm sure Freddie has just got himself tied up with something."

"It's possible," said Pouch. "He might also have been fed through a mincing machine, had his feet encased with concrete and dropped in the sea, or even been abducted by aliens ..."

"I'm afraid I can't help you," said Winnie.

"Now, if you'll excuse me, I'm still feeling a little unwell."

With that, she turned and trotted out of the room.

"Did she sound unwell to you?" Tray asked Pouch.

Pouch shrugged. "A little hoarse, maybe ..." He turned to leave, then froze, staring at a shelf of DVDs. "Look!" he cried. "She's got

"She's got the Hairy Petter box set!"

The dog stretched up to the shelf high above him. Standing on tip-toes he … could … just … about … reach. But, the boxset slipped from his grasp. It fell on top of a golden showjumping trophy below. The award toppled over and, before anyone could catch it, hit an expensive-looking vase, shattering it to pieces.

"Ooops!" Pouch exclaimed. "Butterpaws!"

Tray was about to tell her partner to stop horsing around, when she spotted a switch on the wall that had been hidden behind the vase. "What's this?" she said, pressing the button.

Instantly, there was a loud 'click'.

The wall behind Pouch swung open like a giant door, water sloshing around in the tanks attached to it.

"Pouch!" she hissed. "Look at that!"

The doggy detective turned round. "What?" he cried. "Now someone's stolen a wall!"

"No!" said Tray. "It's the entrance to a secret room. Come on …"

Walking quietly, the pair crept into the hidden room — and found a turtle tied up. Alongside it was a trussed up red-and-blue feathered parrot. He had tape around his beak to keep him quiet.

"Sheldon and Freddie!" exclaimed Tray, rushing over to them. She had just untied

the parrot's wings when she heard another
voice. A low, hissing voice.

"Fi fuffen foo fat fif fi fer foo!"

Tray spun around as Coral the snake
slithered out of the shadows, a horse

tranquiliser gun clenched in her mouth. Her long tongue was wrapped around the trigger.

Pouch tilted his head to one side. "What did you say?"

Coral sighed. "Fi fed ... fi fuffen foo fat fif fi fer foo!"

Pouch shook his head. "Nope. Didn't get it that time, either."

"Maybe you should take the dart gun out of your mouth?" Tray suggested.

"Fo fance!"

Now his wings were free, Freddie reached up and tore the tape from around his beak. "She s-said, I w-wouldn't d-do that if I were you!"

Tray looked stern. "Or else what?"

"Isn't it obvious?" said Pouch. "She'll shoot us, and it will probably really hurt!"

"Or worse," said Tray.

Pouch gulped. "It's all right for you. You've got another eight lives to go yet!"

Coral laughed wickedly as her tongue began to tighten around the weapon's trigger. "Fa! Fa! Fa!"

Just then, Winnie hoofed it into the room. "Sheldon!" she shrieked.

Coral turned to look at the newcomer, and Tray leapt into action. Literally. She jumped into the air, landing hard on the end of the snake's tail. "I got this one from you!" she said to Pouch.

Coral screamed, dropping the gun and causing a large, glittering diamond to shoot out of her throat.

Pouch caught it as it whizzed through the air towards him. "The Blue Moo!"

"C-Coral s-stole it!" cried Freddie. "I saw her do it, and panicked. So, I grabbed the

diamond and came here to hide. She turned up about an hour ago."

"So, you used us to find Freddie because you wanted the diamond back?" said Tray.

Coral sneered. "Yes, and I would have gotten away with it if it wasn't for you pesky detectives! You weren't supposed to get in the way."

Tray grabbed the snake so she couldn't slither away. "Pouch," she said. "Call Sergeant Oinker. Tell him to send a police car to this address."

Pouch slid his phone from his pocket. "And someone to drive it, too?"

Tray smiled and nodded. "I think that would help."

Back at the office, Tray reached out to open the door — and froze. The lettering was there, like always, but now it read:

Tray and Pouch Investigations.

"You repainted the sign!" said the cat

in amazement.

Pouch grinned. "I thought you'd like it."

"I love it!" said Tray, giving her partner a hug.

Pouch pushed the door open, and headed for his desk. "I've also stopped calling you a dame in my diary."

Tray smiled. "That is good news!"

Pouch opened the book. "How do you spell 'sweetcheeks'?"

With a small shake of her head, Tray closed the office door — just as the frosted glass shattered, and a curled-up armadillo clattered to the floor. Pouch and Tray watched as the animal unfurled, a look of sheer terror in its eyes.

"Pouch! Tray!" the armadillo cried.
"Someone's after me! You have to help!"

Pouch stood, slamming his diary closed.
"Ready, partner?"

Tray's mouth twisted into a determined
sneer. "I was born ready!"